# SWAPS

# SWAPS

by

*Anthony Smith*

As told on *Jackanory*

Illustrated by Jan Brychta

BBC Books

*For Quintin, with love.*

Published by BBC Books,
a division of BBC Enterprises Limited,
Woodlands, 80 Wood Lane, London W12 0TT
First published 1992
© Anthony Smith 1992
ISBN 0 563 36314 2
Illustrations by Jan Brychta
Set in 12/15pt. Century Old Style Roman by Goodfellow & Egan, Cambridge
Printed and bound in Great Britain by Clays Ltd, St Ives PLC
Cover printed by Clays Ltd, St Ives PLC

# CONTENTS

Hump and Duke 7
Tarts and Pies 27
Nincomwolves and Nincompigs 43
Spelling Right and Wrong 59
Oh Tweedle! 75

# Hump
# and
# Duke

It was another day for Humpty Dumpty. He sat on the wall just knowing what was going to happen. It had happened so many times before that he was getting fed up, particularly as it hadn't been nice even on the first occasion. What can possibly be nice about falling and landing on your head? Or landing on your back or on your side? The trouble about being egg-shaped is that a landing anywhere is bad news. Worse still, having fallen, there is the extra problem of being all untogether.

Considerable help, such as that given by the King's horses or, better still, the King's men, is just not able to make things right.

"Woe is me," he said. "Or rather, woe will be me

the moment I fall off."

Just at that moment, as a major change in the daily routine, he heard the sound of marching feet. There were drums as well, and fifes, all making a quite tremendous noise. Humpty decided to stay where he was as the noise was far too exciting to be interrupted by falling off a wall. He knew the sound that King's horses and King's men make, but this marching noise was far finer. And the music was terrific, with its boom-boom-boom and its whistle-whistle-whistle and its pipe-pipe-pipe.

"Oh, but this is wonderful," he said, nearly falling off in his excitement.

The first of the marching men then appeared round the corner. They looked superb in their uniforms and there were dozens of them. Soon came a band,

booming and whistling and piping, and then lots more men, perhaps hundreds this time.

Humpty grew more excited, nearly falling lots more times, but he managed to remember how awful that was, not just falling but landing and being all untogether.

"Hurrah, hurrah," he shouted at the soldiers, as more of them marched by.

Of course Humpty lost count. Even *all* the King's horses and *all* the King's men had never been so many. He thought there must be thousands of the soldiers, perhaps ten thousand in all. What a sight they made, and what a sound with the booming and whistling and piping keeping them all in step. March, march, march around his wall, and then up the hill. It was quite magnificent.

Then there came a man with an even better uniform than the others. How proud he must be, as he was obviously in charge. How important he was, with such a uniform. And how grand he looked as he marched, marched, marched in time with that boom, boom, boom and pipe, whistle, pipe. Humpty could see the man was muttering to himself, and soon was near enough to hear.

"Woe is me," he said. "Or rather woe will be me when I reach the hill and have to start marching up it."

"What do you mean 'Woe'?" asked Humpty Dumpty. "In all my experience of the military I have never seen such a wonderful body of men. There must be ten thousand of them."

"There *are* ten thousand," said the man in the beautiful uniform. "That's the trouble. There are never ten thousand and one or nine thousand, nine hundred and ninety-nine. It's always ten thousand and always up the hill."

"It seems like a pretty good number to me," said Humpty Dumpty, "and what on earth's wrong about going up a lovely hill, particularly with all that booming and banging?"

"I don't mind going up," said the man. "It's having to come down again that I don't like."

"It should be easier coming down," said Humpty, who then remembered that falling down was no fun at all. "At least you don't fall," he added.

"No, I don't fall," said the man, "but I wish at times I did, as it would make a nice change, instead of just marching up and marching down again."

"Why don't you all stop and look at the view?" asked Humpty. "Perhaps when you're half-way up?"

"Oh, we couldn't do that," he replied. "Besides, when we're half-way up we're neither up nor down."

This *was* puzzling. Humpty Dumpty had never thought much about being half-way. With him, when half-way between the top of the wall and the ground, he was too busy worrying which bit of him was going to hit first.

"What's your name?" he suddenly asked the soldier.

"Well, it's a bit of a long name really. You see I'm the Duke of York, and sometimes people call me Grand, which I do like, and Old, which I don't like so much."

"So you're the Duke of York Grand Old," said Humpty, who was a bit confused.

"No, it's the other way about," said the soldier.

"You mean it's the Old Grand York of Duke?"

"Absolutely not," said the soldier, now getting cross as Old Grand soldiers sometimes do.

"Well, you're the Grand York of Old Duke, or the Old York of Grand Duke, or the York Duke of Old . . ."

The soldier interrupted, having had enough.

"I'm no more any of those than you are Dumpty Humpty. I'll have you know that I'm the Grand Old Duke of York. At least I'm fairly Grand and not terribly Old, but I do have ten thousand men, and I march them up the hill, again and again."

Now this was interesting to Humpty Dumpty.

14

Firstly the man knew his name. Secondly it was terribly exciting to meet someone who did something so interesting. How wonderful it must be to march with ten thousand men up and down the hill.

"It's awfully tiring," said the Duke, "just marching, marching, marching, up, down, and half-way up the hill. Quite frankly, I'd like to sit by myself sometimes, just like you do."

"Not half as much as I'd like to go marching up a hill," said Humpty Dumpty.

"Well, why don't we swap?" replied the Grand Old Duke.

"Terrific," said Humpty, "and what's wrong with now?"

The Duke immediately jumped on the wall. Then, carefully, he lowered Humpty down. It was the first time Humpty had ever reached the ground without

breaking apart. It was also the first time the Duke had sat on a wall. Both of them were quite ecstatic about their new situations. Humpty rushed off up the hill. The Duke rushed nowhere, and just sat.

"Don't forget to get to the top of the hill," he shouted.

"And don't forget to fall off," Humpty shouted back as he puffed and panted to keep up with the others, the ten thousand others.

Now, we all know, particularly those of us who are a bit egg-shaped, that it's quite difficult walking up a hill. And Humpty Dumpty was very, very egg-shaped. Worse still, the ten thousand men were used to marching upwards, and downwards, and they didn't get puffed a bit. Humpty became more and

more behind. In fact, when the others were all at the top of the hill, he was only half-way up. And when they were all at the bottom, he was only half-way down. He thought of rolling, as egg-shaped is almost ball-shaped, but he wondered if he mightn't break before he reached the bottom. Then there would be the same old trouble with King's men and King's horses failing to put him together again. No, it was better to stay where he was, and try and catch up with the men when they were next passing him.

As for the Grand Old Duke of York he was very happy sitting on the wall. It was the nicest thing he had ever sat on. It was comfortable. There was a leafy tree nearby. And he could just hear the ten thousand men, marching, marching to the drum, drum, and fife, fife, and whistle, whistle. How nice it was, he thought, to be doing nothing of the kind.

"You do look silly sitting up there," said a small voice right behind him.

The Duke looked round at once, and saw a young girl.

"You do look *very* silly," she said again. "What's an old soldier like you doing sitting on a wall? Shouldn't you be marching up a hill or something?"

The Duke of York's happiness vanished at once. It had been bad enough Humpty Dumpty getting his name wrong. Now there was this little girl saying he looked silly, and old, and apparently not grand at all.

"I'm the Grand Old Duke of York, I'll have you know," he said, drawing himself up to his full height. Or as much as he could while still sitting down.

17

"Well," said the little girl, who was being a bit nasty, "you don't look very grand to me, or like a duke, but I agree about the old part."

This made him so angry, as old grand soldiers sometimes are, that he drew his sword and had every intention of sticking it into her. But she jumped away and he, most ungrandly, fell off the wall. Just at that moment, having seen the fall, a party of the King's horses and King's men came galloping up.

"But this isn't right," they said after seeing it wasn't Humpty Dumpty lying on the ground. "We're supposed to put together an egg-shaped Humpty and not some kind of old soldier."

"Silly some kind of old soldier," said the nasty little girl.

Poor Grand Old Duke of York. He was not only furious but wounded from his fall, and – worse still – had his sword mixed with his legs, so that he couldn't stab anybody, such as the little girl.

Then came a strange rumbling from the nearby hill. It wasn't a marching noise. It wasn't a drum or fife or whistle noise. It was the sort of noise you would expect from something egg-shaped rolling downwards very fast. Poor Humpty had missed his footing when going either up or down – he wasn't certain which – but he knew he was hurtling downwards.

"Help – *squelch* – hellp – *bounce* – helllp – *squash* – hellllp!" he called, and his egg-shape became square-shaped and then banana-shaped and every-other-

kind-of-shape as he bounced, tumbled, cannoned, and
generally rolled downhill.

Eventually he smashed into a wall, his wall, as
untogether as he had ever been.

"Ah," said the King's men. "Now we can get on
with it, as we're supposed to put a Humpty together,
not an old soldier, even if he has fallen off a wall."

"Silly old soldier," said the nasty girl, "and
silly old Humpty too. Now no one will be able to help
me."

"I wouldn't help you even if I could," said the Duke,
trying to reach his sword again.

"What about helping me?" groaned Humpty. "I'm as untogether as can be."

"Well, I might," said the girl, "if you will help me find my sheep."

"Are they up a hill?" asked Humpty, still groaning.

"Perhaps, but probably not," she said.

"You mean we won't have to march up and down if we help?" grumped the Duke, annoyed even that he was speaking to her.

"No marching," she said. "No sitting on walls. No falling off walls. No waiting to be put together again.

All you have to do is find my sheep."

"It sounds wonderful," said Humpty Dumpty.

"It doesn't sound so bad," muttered the Duke.

"What's your name?" they both asked together.

"Bo Peep," she said, "but you can call me Bo if you like."

"Oh, and you can call me Hump if you like," said Hump.

"And I'll even let you call me Duke," said the Duke.

So, in time, when thoroughly mended, the three of them set off, Hump, Duke and Bo.

After a time Bo decided she was fed up looking for her sheep. After all, she had been looking for them for as long as she could remember. Duke and Hump seemed so happy at their new job that she could leave them to it.

"You'll know my sheep," she told them, "because they'll be wagging their tails behind them."

Then she turned on her heels and left her two new friends. If the truth be known what she now wanted to find wasn't so much sheep as soldiers. There had been ten thousand of them with the silly old Duke of York. And there had been *all* the King's men, and their horses, with silly old Hump. She thought they would be much more interesting than any number of sheep. And far more interesting than one old Duke and an egg-shaped Dumpty.

At that moment Bo heard the piping and the drumming, and she began to run. Duke and Hump also began to run because, at that same moment, they heard some distant bleating.

"What fun if we find the sheep," they said.

"What fun if I find the soldiers," thought Miss Peep.

As to whether sheep or soldiers *are* more fun, well, that's another story.

# Tarts
# and
# Pies

It was a bright and sunny day at the Palace. It always was bright and sunny at palaces. This was because those in them were usually living happily ever after, and you can't expect people such as kings and queens to live happily ever after if it's raining. No, it has to be sunny and bright and just the kind of day for, well, doing a bit of cooking.

As we all know the Queen of Hearts particularly liked making tarts. What none of us knows is what Jack did after he had done the deed for which he is so famous. We've never heard of the Jack of Hearts doing anything else except stealing tarts. So he must have been very keen on them, and liked the sticky jam too much to spread it around on books, doors, table-tops and arm-chairs like some other people do.

Well, truth to tell, he only liked a few. He always stole them all, but each time – having gobbled half-a-dozen greedily – he realised that a man can have too many tarts, even a tart-thief such as our Jack. So he usually sat down, looked at the tarts he didn't want, and did nothing with them. Then when the Queen made some more, he just had to steal those as well. And then, once again, he would wonder why he had taken so many.

"There must be more to life than tarts," he muttered to himself, and then had a BRILLIANT idea. Why didn't he exchange his surplus tarts for other kinds of food? Perhaps other people were as fed up as he was, but fed up with different food. Such as roast beef. Or peanut butter sandwiches. Or chip butties. As it was a bright and sunny day, like always, he set off to find some other food, something he had never done before.

A short while later he saw a little girl fairly shovelling it in.

He couldn't see what she was eating, but as sure as eggs are eggs it wasn't tarts. Never had he seen anybody quite so busy with a ladle. In fact he had never seen such a ladle or such an enormous bowl. Just at that moment she leaped up, leaving her as-sure-as-eggs-are-eggs-it-wasn't-tarts where she had been sitting. The Jack of Hearts, always fairly nimble on his feet, hurried over, amazed at his good fortune.

"Can I help?" he asked, trying to get a better look

at the as-sure-as-eggs-are-eggs now that he was nearer.

"Do you like spiders?" she asked by way of reply.

It couldn't be, thought Jack. Was she really eating spiders? And with such a huge ladle?

"Well, do you?" she asked again.

"Not particularly," he said, looking nervously at the bowl in case one crept out of it.

"Well, I absolutely hate them," she said, "and I'd be very grateful if you'd chase the one away that has just come down."

Jack heaved a great big sigh. Of course he would chase it away. And then he might be allowed to have a go at the bowl.

"Have a tart," he said abruptly, after chasing off the spider.

31

"No, thank you very much," she replied, ever so correctly. "I'd rather get back to my curds and whey."

"Your curds and what?" he asked.

"My curds and whey, silly. The curds are the cheesy bit of the milk and the whey is the watery bit that isn't the cheesy bit."

Jack was appalled. A bowl full of spiders suddenly seemed quite nice. Could her curds and whatever look as bad as it sounded? He peeped into the bowl. It was worse than it sounded with great globs of lumpy milk swimming in yellowish water. He suddenly felt sick. Quite a lot sick. And a terrible thought came into his mind that that was what had happened to her. His legs gave way beneath him, and he sat down on a tuffet.

'Would you like your tart back?" she asked, still ever so sweetly, before putting her ladle into the bowl and opening her mouth wide.

Jack couldn't wait a moment longer. He got up, and ran away far faster than he ever did from the Queen when he raided her kitchen. He ran and ran, and only slowed down on seeing a nice old couple having a meal outside their house. Perhaps they would like a tart, he thought, and he could then have a little of what they were serving up.

"Some more lean, Mr Sprat?" said the lady.

"Only if you'll have a little more fat," said the man in reply.

The Jack of Hearts began to feel ill all over again. The lady took a great piece of fat, cut a big bit out of

it, and opened her mouth wide. Once again Jack couldn't wait a moment longer. Once more he ran faster than he ever did from the Queen. He ran even faster than he had done from that little girl with the bowl of cheesy, watery, lumpy milk. He didn't know anyone could run so fast, but then he didn't know anyone ate such things. Surely somebody somewhere was eating something that didn't make him feel ill just by looking at it. Eventually he slowed down, quite out of breath.

"Oh, I am good," said a voice from behind a hedge. "What a good boy am I!"

Very cautiously the Jack of Hearts peered over the hedge. After all it had been a difficult day, and he didn't feel like taking any more risks.

So he looked and saw a fat boy sitting in the corner between two hedges. More importantly – by far – he

saw a pie that was almost as fat as the boy. It looked delicious. It looked scrumptious. Better still, such a pie-looking pie couldn't possibly contain curds and what, or fat, or even spiders. It just had to be full of good things, pie-ish things that were probably even better than tarts.

At that moment the fat boy stuck his fat thumb into the fat pie. Amazingly, just with that thumb, he pulled out one plum.

"What a good boy am I!" he said, all over again.

What kind of ding-dong have we got here? thought Jack to himself. What sort of jerk can consider himself good just because he has stuck his ugly great thumb into a lovely-looking pie? It may be a touch clever to extract one plum with one thumb, but it's nothing to shout about.

As the pie did look terrific, even with ugly thumbholes in it, Jack decided to speak to him and discover if he was half as baked as his pie.

"Hello," said the Jack of Hearts, "would you care for a tart?"

"Not many plums in them," said the ding-dong.

"No," replied Jack, "but they're quite good for sticking thumbs in."

"No point in thumb-sticking," said the jerk, "if there's no hope of plum-pulling."

The Jack of Hearts immediately felt like moving on, but the un-thumbed part of the pie did look even better the more he looked at it.

"What kind of pie is it?" he asked.

"It's a Christmas pie, of course," said the thumb-skull, being more irritating than ever.

Jack had no idea what a Christmas pie contained, apart from the odd plum that an even odder boy could gouge out from time to time. Perhaps this individual was the famous Tom Thumb he had heard about, except that Tom Thumb was supposed to be small and this one was, in a word, fat. Or, in two words, very fat. So perhaps he was the equally famous Simple Simon, who was not only simple but keen on pies. He had deliberately met a pie-man going to the fair, even if he didn't get the pie in the old story.

"So what's your name?" asked the Jack of Hearts.

"Jack," said the pie-holder.

"It can't be; I'm Jack," said the Jack of Hearts.

"Well, I am, and after Jack comes Horner. What comes after your Jack?" he asked.

"Hearts," said the Jack of Hearts, who felt they were getting away from the important subject. "What is in a Christmas pie?" he added.

"Plums, of course," said Jack Horner. "At least, I never find anything else when I stick in my thumb, and finding plums is good enough for me."

The thumb-sticker then stuck his thumb in the tart he had been offered, and the Jack of Hearts hated him tremendously. That was no way to treat a decent tart, particularly one made by a Queen, and freshly stolen that very day.

"No plums," said the plum-skull. "How can I possibly say that I'm a good boy if there are no plums? Take your beastly tart away, I won't have any tart today."

The Jack of Hearts didn't run away this time. He just walked away, feeling very sad. Not only had he been given none of that delicious pie, but one of his tarts had been ruined by that terrible thumb. At least the girl with the curds and the couple with the fat had been polite, but the miserable Horner deserved to be stuck in his own pie. What a good boy I would be if only I could do that, thought the Jack of Hearts. That would be more fun than stealing tarts.

Wearily, he trudged back to the Palace. It was still bright and sunny, of course. It always was. Why couldn't there be rain for a change? Or, better still, thunder and lightning? Or snow and hail, or sleet and gale? The Jack of Hearts was in a terrible mood, sad and hungry, and hurt and angry, all wrapped into one. He had only wanted to swap some of his tarts for other people's food. And all he had got was rudeness and the sight, and smell, of food he didn't know existed, such as a bowl of curd and a plate of fat. But the pie had looked good, and the thought of that made him even sadder, and angrier, and hungrier.

Suddenly, in front of him, and walking to the Palace, was a man carrying something looking suspiciously like a pie. It can't be, thought Jack. You don't get to see two pies in a single day. The man was singing, something about sixpence, when Jack caught up with him.

"What's that you've got?"

"Pie," said the man.

"Who's it for?" asked Jack.

"King," said the man.

This was terrific, thought Jack. A pie fit for the King. This would be better than tarts, and a million times better than curds and whatever and fat. The pie

smelt wonderful. It had to be wonderful. It would be wonderful. Together he and the pie-carrier walked into the Palace, and the sun seemed to shine more brightly than ever. Straight into the royal chamber went the pie-man, and the dish was set before the King. Someone produced a knife, and Jack wondered how big a slice he might get once the King had had his go. It did look the daintiest dish that ever he had seen.

Jack was slobbering and very happy when the knife was plunged into that pie. He was still slobbering and still happy when he heard a tweet coming from underneath its delicious-looking crust. By the time he had heard twenty-four tweets his slobbering had absolutely stopped. So had his happiness. When he

saw the first black and feathery head he wondered if
he would ever be able to slobber again – at anything.
By the time he had seen twenty-four black and
feathery heads he began to think that globs of curd
swimming in cheesy milk weren't so bad after all.
What could be worse than a blackbird pie, a tweeting,
living blackbird pie, a twenty-four-tweeting, living
blackbird pie?

Jack felt like being sick, and knew at once what
would be worse than a twenty-four-tweeting, living
blackbird pie. But he managed not to be sick all over
it.

In fact he just managed not to be sick at all by
hurrying out of the royal chamber and into the
parlour. There was the Queen putting flour and sugar
and jam and butter on a table, just as she always did.
And, when the time came, he stole her tarts, just as
he always did. And, once again, he ate half-a-dozen
before wondering why he always stole so many. But

at least they were better than curds and what. And
much better than fat. And tremendously much better
than blackbirds, tweet or no tweet. Besides, he could
eat them with his thumb. He wanted to practise
eating this way. When he was really good at thumbing
pies, good enough to pull out a plum, he would get
back at that loathsome Horner. He would pull out lots
of plums before the fat little boy could stop him. Oh
what fun, Jack thought, if he could be better than
Horner. What a good boy I will be!

# Nincomwolves
# and
# Nincompigs

"I don't know about you," said one wolf to another one day, "but I feel we have a bad reputation."

"What's a *repatation*?" asked the other wolf, who knew words like pig and food but wasn't so good on longer ones.

"A reputation is what other people say about you," said the first wolf, "and they say that we're big and bad."

"So they should," said the other wolf, "because we are big and we are bad."

"That's not the point," said the more intelligent wolf. "It would be better if we had a good reputation. Then we could trick others more easily, such as pigs."

"Oh, I see what you mean," said the second wolf, even if he had no idea how you start being good.

It seemed about as difficult as to start being little if you happen to be big.

"How do we do that?" he asked. "How on earth does a big bad wolf become a little good one?"

This was a tricky question, even for a wolf who knew words like intelligent. But he thought and thought, and realised that most people didn't actually meet wolves. They only heard about them, and the bad things they heard got worse and worse as more and more people told the stories. So what was wanted were some good stories, and then wolves would become more and more good the more that people told these stories.

"It's all to do with exaggeration," he said.

"What's *exarregation*?" replied the other wolf, wondering why anyone used such long words when short ones like pig and food and wolf and bad were quite good enough.

"I'll tell you about exarregation, I mean exgaggeration, or whatever the word is," said the first wolf, "by reminding you of that stupid little girl who was taking some food to her grandmother. And about her equally stupid grandmother who opened the door for a wolf thinking it was the little girl. Any grandmother who makes that kind of mistake deserves to be eaten. As for a girl who thinks, even for a second, that a wolf lying in bed is a grandmother – well, she deserves to be eaten too. So we wolves are actually helping by removing such nincompoops from the scene. And what do we get in return? A bad reputation, that's what we get. Grandmothers and little girls can talk of nothing else except wolves, and how big and bad we are and how no one should take food to grandmothers any more. So grandmothers are waiting in bed, all over the place, for food that never comes. And everything is said to be our fault . . .

"I know what," he added. "We'll start a food distribution service."

"What's *distrubition*?" asked the other one, and then shut up on seeing more teeth snarling than he had ever seen before.

"We'll get a couple of riding hoods," said the first wolf, once his snarl had died down. "Everyone who takes food to grandmothers seems to wear a riding hood, and we want to do it properly. In that way we'll improve our reputation like anything."

So they found baskets and hoods, stole some food – well, how else were they to get it? – and set off to

visit some grandmothers. At the very first house they knocked ever so gently, and explained to the granny inside how they had brought some food for her.

"What kind of nincomgran do you take me for?" she shouted back. "Don't think your riding hoods fool me because I know you are wolves, big bad wolves."

The two wolves backed away, with their tails between their legs, to find another house with a grandmother inside. It's not easy getting a good reputation, they thought, but were determined to succeed.

At the next house they left the basket of food outside the door, and then retreated. From a distance they shouted:

"Hello, grandmother, there's some food for you if you care to open up."

"You must be a couple of nincomwolves if you think I'll fall for that one," said the voice from within. "There's obviously one of you just waiting to pounce, and then you'll gobble me up. So be off with you." And off went the wolves, once again, their tails further between their legs.

Fortunately the forest was full of little old houses with little old grandmothers inside. Soon they were in front of another. The wolves decided this time just to leave the food and say nothing. The grandmother would notice it, they agreed, when she came out to pick mushrooms, chop down trees, or do whatever

grandmothers do when they're not being beastly to wolves. Later that day they crept back to the house to see if the basket had been taken. It hadn't. It was still where they had left it. They approached closer still, ever so quietly.

Suddenly, from right above, came a most tremendous noise. And then sticks and stones pelted down at them. *Crash. Bang. Wallop.* More *crash.* More *bang.* More *wallop.*

"Be gone with you!" shouted a voice from the trees. "I won't be caught by your stupid trick. Just because I'm a grandmother you think you can fool me, do you? Well, be gone."

The two wolves, rained on by the sticks and stones, caught a glimpse of a grandmother up a tree, and were off. It was no time for explanation. All they had wanted was to give some food. And what they got in return were a couple of sore heads, and sore bodies, and a couple of sore ears from all the words she hurled at them.

"Nincomwolves," she yelled. "Stupid thought-you'd-be-ever-so-clever big bad wolves."

Poor wolves. Poor bruised wolves. Poor bruised tails-between-their-legs-further-than-ever wolves. And they had only tried to be kind to some nasty, spiteful, suspicious, stone-throwing, jabbering grandmothers. Instead of being eaten as they should have been, those grandmothers were probably now spreading the story that wolves were being more cunning, and therefore bigger and badder than ever before.

Just at that moment a little pig wandered by. It saw the wolves and ran squealing into a bush. The wolves couldn't be bothered to chase it, which amazed the little pig.

"Aren't you supposed to be huffing and puffing?" he said, "and shouldn't you be going on about the hairs on your chinny-chin-chin?"

The wolves were not interested, and said so. The little pig, still hiding in the bush, began to get annoyed.

"You're supposed to be interested," he said. "And you're supposed to huff and puff and blow our houses down. Surely you know that? We make a house of straw and you blow that down. Then we make one of sticks and you blow that down. And, finally, we make one of bricks, and you can't blow it down."

"That's always struck me as being such a stupid story, and quite out of character," said the more intelligent wolf.

"What's out of *charctarer*?" said the other wolf.

"It means," said the first wolf, snarling quite a lot, "that we don't go around blowing houses down to get our food. Besides we can't huff and puff very well, and couldn't blow a house down if it was made of tissue paper. If we want to eat a pig we just catch one, and we don't blow down houses any more than we dress up as grandmothers or talk about the hairs on our chinny-chin-chins. It's all quite ridiculous."

"What's ri—," said the other wolf, stopping just in time.

"Ever since I've been a little pig," said the little pig,

"I have been told that wolves are big and bad, and blow down houses, and end up coming down chimneys and getting boiled."

The wolves shuddered at the thought. They didn't like anything about the story, particularly its ending. Of course they knew it, just as everybody else did, and that was the trouble. It gave them such a bad name.

"I know," said the intelligent wolf, "let's swap the story round a bit, just as we tried to do with those nasty old grandmothers. Let's help a pig to make a house, and then see what people have to say."

"Great," said the other wolf who, for once, had understood every single word.

It took them quite a bit of time to persuade the little pig to come out of the bush. Both wolves had to stand at a distance, cover up their eyes, and promise to count to ten before the little pig dared to come out and collect his two brothers. This little pig then spent quite a time persuading them that the wolves had been hit on the head, by some stick or stone, as they had gone bonkers, daft, and off their nuts because they were even offering to build houses for pigs.

"Who do they think we are?" queried the other little pigs, "Nincompigs?"

"It's true, it's true," said the first little pig. "They want to build us homes."

At that moment the two wolves arrived.

"Are you really going to build us homes?" asked the pigs, all speaking together.

"Yup," said the wolves, "and what shall we make them with?"

"What about straw?" said the first pig.

"Straw's no good," said the wiser wolf. "The first puff of wind will blow it down."

"What about sticks?" asked the second little pig.

"Sticks are no good," said the wolf. "The wind blows straight through sticks, and a stick-house is about as cosy as sitting in a hedge."

"What about bricks then?" said the third little pig.

"Now you're talking," said the wolf. "You're talking sense, you're talking wisdom, you're talking bricks."

All five of them then set to work, the two wolves and the three pigs.

They dug up clay, baked it, piled the bricks on top

of each other, added windows and doors, and soon had a fine house. They put 'Dungruntin' over the front door, and the five of them felt terribly pleased with themselves.

While they had been working others had been astonished by the sight of pigs and wolves cooperating.

"Never seen anything like it," they said. "Whatever will happen next? Pigs flying? Cows jumping over the moon? Dishes running away with spoons? Who could tell?"

The three pigs all settled into the one house, which was much better than having a house each. The occasional grandmother passed by, muttering that it wasn't natural, and that no good would come of it, but did admit it was a sight for sore eyes. Soon the pigs felt hungry. So they snuffled about outside, dug up some roots with their noses, ate those roots, ate some nuts they found, and apples, and acorns, and then more roots, and more nuts, and felt so much better that they went to sleep. Their little round bodies snuggled up next to each other, and all three breathed together.

Soon the wolves also felt hungry. They had watched the pigs eating the roots, the nuts, the apples, the acorns, the second lot of nuts and of roots, and wondered how anybody could eat such things. What they wanted was, well, something like a fat little pig. In fact something very like one of the three little bodies all snoozing away, snuggled up together and looking so very, very edible.

"We can't do that," said the wiser wolf. "It will spoil our new reputation."

"No, we can't," said the other wolf. "It would spoil whatever it was you just said."

So they sighed, and tried to go to sleep. But they were too hungry, and the little pigs looked increasingly edible with every minute that passed.

Just then a grandmother went by.

"Don't ever trust a wolf," she cried out, "they're all big and bad and now they're being cunning as well."

"It sounds," said the second wolf, "as if we haven't done our repetition any good."

"Reputation," said the wiser wolf, "but it seems as if you're right – for once."

"Don't trust them," came the voice from outside. "They're still wolves."

"Oh well," they both said, "perhaps she's right."

So they gobbled up all three little pigs. That done, and because she was still shouting, they ate the grandmother. On their way home they met two other grandmothers and gobbled them up as well. Then they met a silly little girl in a red riding hood, and ate her up.

"Let's face it," they said, as they curled up in a nice warm den, "in all the fairy stories the wolves are always big and bad. So we might as well be as big and bad as possible."

With that they chuckled to each other, patted their round bellies, went to sleep and dreamed and dreamed about lots and lots more fat little pigs.

# Spelling
# Right
# and
# Wrong

Once upon a time there lived a man who was the
neatest and tidiest person in the whole world.
His clothes were always beautifully pressed. His
shoes were shiny. His socks never slipped down. Of
course his shirt was well tucked into his trousers. His
bed was always neat. The cushions were always in
their right place. And there was never any food left
over from each meal. He always knew what he
wanted, cooked what he wanted, and therefore ate it
all up. The washing-up was done the moment each
meal was over.

Everything outside his house was just as neat and
tidy. The path was as straight as a ruler. The
flower-beds were absolutely rectangular, and even

the flowers were arranged in rows according to size and according to colour. He hated it when they dropped their petals, because that meant untidiness until he tidied them. He even wondered why smoke couldn't come straight out of his ever-so-straight chimneys. And why did the birds, looking for worms on his immaculate grass, walk about any-old-how and not in line?

His nearest neighbour was nothing like as neat and tidy as he was – well, who could be? – but she did her best. She lived in a shoe, which made things difficult for her, but it was a smart shoe, and she cleaned it every day. Whenever she felt like visiting him she would spend a couple of hours getting herself ready. She knew how he hated a single hair to be out of place, and she combed and combed and brushed and brushed until she was as perfect as could be. Only then did she walk up the very centre of the very straight path that led towards his house.

"Hello," she would say, "I hope I'm not disturbing you."

"Not at all," he would reply, perhaps flicking a brand-new speck of dust off his shoulder or hurrying to catch a petal which had chosen that moment to fall.

She only quite liked visiting him because she was so afraid of doing something terrible, like dropping a crumb or moving a plate.

"Today, we are lucky," he said one day. "Today we have cake as I found a sixpence down by the stile."

"Oh good," she said, worrying like anything that it

might be a crumbly cake and awkward to eat.

Unfortunately it was an extremely difficult cake. He was trying to cut a beautifully slice-shaped slice when a piece of the icing broke off. He grabbed for it and upset the sugar-bowl. He grabbed for the sugar-bowl, where all the lumps had been neatly stacked, and his well-pressed sleeve knocked the milk jug. Oh dear, what a mess! There was milk and sugar and cake everywhere. A blackbird arrived and took a beakful. Other birds arrived, excited by the hubbub, and the man groaned and moaned in his despair.

"Oh I wish, I wish," he said, "this sort of thing didn't happen. Why can't everything always be neat and tidy?"

Then, so saddened by the mess, he burst into

tears. This distressed the shoe-house lady terribly. She got out her hankie to wipe his tears, but remembered she had already used it – and on her nose. That would never do. But what would do? How could she cheer him up?

Well, a long time ago she had bought a book of spells. She had been lonely in her home, and had looked up a friendship spell, but something had gone wrong. She had just wanted company, and had asked for it, but then got a plague of spiders. So she had boiled yet another dead toad, as that was an ingredient, before reading the spell again, but being much more careful with the words.

"Oh flattened toad,
  Squashed on the road,
  Bring me a friend to share my shoe,
  Someone good-looking, yes please do."

Once again it didn't work. She had got a lot of mice, who were quite nice-looking, but they weren't what she had in mind. Then came quite a nice-looking cat, but it only ate up the nice-looking mice before going on its way. Spells, as she had learned, were difficult.

"Boo-hoo," said the man even more noisily, and she knew she had to do something. She racked her brains for a suitable spell. Oh, please, oh please, she said to herself. And then she remembered, or rather she thought she did, but in any case it was worth a try. All the birds flew off when she started, ever so loudly, and lots of petals fell.

"Hocus pocus, Out of focus,
  Jiggery-pokey, Help this blokey,
  Let his wish come quite true,
  Abracadabra, yes please do."

Talk about bangs! Talk about lightning and puffs of smoke! There was even a smell of sulphur in the air. To begin with the poor lady was too frightened to open her eyes. But then the smoke got up her nose. She coughed and spluttered, and wondered if she wasn't on fire. So she just had to look.

"Glory be!" she said. "Lor luvaduck! Bless my soul. Strewth!"

"Could you inform me more precisely what has occurred?" said the man, who always did speak a bit differently and had now stopped crying.

"Stone the crows," she said, "Od's bodkins. Bob's your uncle. Blow me."

"Despite your fluent description I am still somewhat at a loss," said the man.

"Well, look at yourself," she said. And he did. A more crumpled sight he had never seen. His suit was all creased. His hat was all bent. His shoes and trousers went every-which-way, and everything was as crooked as could be, his house, his garden path, his chimneys, and even the old stile at the corner of the field.

"I think I must have got it a bit wrong," she said. "I never was a good speller."

For a moment, a very long moment, the man didn't know what to say. He looked at his walking-stick. It was as wiggly as could be. He looked at the table and chairs. There wasn't a straight line to them. He looked at his flowers, and they grew at every angle save the vertical. Just then a cat, with a very crooked tail, chased an equally crooked mouse right through

the flower-bed. He was about to protest, as surely he would have done before, but then realised there was nothing to protest about. The flowers were as disorderly as could be, with or without the cat charging through them. It didn't matter any longer. So he even laughed when the crooked cat and crooked mouse ran right back again. At first it was just a little laugh. Then it became a huge, great, gallumphing, guffaw of a laugh, the sort of laugh he didn't know he had in him, or could come out of him.

The lady also hadn't known he could make such a noise. A polite little chuckle was all she had heard. But she was enormously relieved that he wasn't unhappy about becoming so terribly, gawkily, contortedly, knottedly, crooked. His cuffs were like no cuffs had ever been. His clothes were more of a jigsaw than any form of suit. His nose didn't know which way to go. His ears stuck out, and she couldn't decide which one was odder than the other.

"You do look, well, different," she said.

"I am different," he said, "decidedly so, and happily so."

With that he leapt up, and instantly fell over. His crooked stick had let him down, but he was still laughing as he lay on the crooked path in the middle of the crookedest garden that ever you did see.

"How did this happen?" he asked, when he had wobbled to his feet.

"It was all my fault," she said. "I was trying to help, but I think I got the wrong spell."

"You didn't," he laughed. "You got it more right than anyone could have done. I love being crooked, and I don't have to care any more about things being out of line. It's wonderful. Just look at that smoke coming from the chimney. It doesn't care where it goes, and nor do I. It's all quite wonderful."

She was very happy that he was happy. And also a little proud that her spell had been so effective, even if not quite what she had intended.

"I didn't know you could do spells," he said, as if reading her thoughts.

"Well, I can't really," she said. "At least I try them from time to time but I never seem to get them right."

"Oh yes, you do, yes, you do," he said. "But what

69

about yourself? Haven't you ever tried to give yourself anything?"

She was a bit ashamed to answer him correctly. She couldn't very well tell him that she had wanted company, particularly as he was just across the field. But she hadn't wanted *his* company. He was so finicky. Or rather he had been so finicky and tidying things all the time. He certainly hadn't been the kind of company she had wanted.

"Come on," he asked again, "surely there's something you have wanted for yourself?"

"Yes," she replied, but very hesitantly, "I had wanted to, well, look after somebody in my shoe-home."

"Oh I see," he said, "you wanted a child."

"Yes, that's it," she said hurriedly, "I wanted a child, but of course that would be a bit difficult."

"Spells can do anything," said the man. "Look what they did to me. What spell do you have to say to get a child?"

She couldn't remember. After all, she had only asked for company before, for good-looking company. You would have to say something quite different for a child.

"Come on," said the crooked man, most impatiently.

"Shh," she said, "I've got to think."

And think she did, muttering to herself.

"'Witch's broom-sticks, burst appendix', – oh no, that's for getting well. 'Squashed tomato, yolk of egg, chipped potato, broken leg,' – oh dear, I can't remember what that's for."

And then, quite suddenly, she did remember. Very slowly, and carefully (because she didn't want another mistake), she spoke the words.

"Hocus Pocus, all you jokers,
  Hear the number I have dialled.
  Six pints of bitter, and eight of mild,
  Please deliver me one child."

"Please deliver me one child," said the man, echoing her words.

"Yes, please deliver me one child," she said, before saying it again and again and again as she realised what fun that would be. "Please, please, please," she said, "a child, a child, a child."

But nothing happened. Not a bang. No lightning or smoke. Not even the faintest whiff of sulphur.

"Oh well," said the lady, who was feeling very sad, "I think I'll go home now. Sorry about the cake."

"I'll walk you home," said the man, who had never said that sort of thing before.

The two of them went slowly down the crooked path and came to the crooked stile. He was helping her over it when he saw a sixpence lying on the ground.

"What luck," he said, "another sixpence!"

She laughed on seeing it was crooked, and said it was even luckier to find a crooked coin. As they walked across the field towards her home they suddenly heard lots of noise. It wasn't bird noise, but did sound a bit like birds, lots of them, squabbling perhaps over food, squawking and shrieking, whistling and piping. The man and woman even ran,

so keen were they to discover what was making all that sound.

And then they saw. There were children everywhere. Some were coming out of the top of the shoe, some through the lace-holes, and some were sliding off the toe. What a noise! What a caterwauling!

"What fun," said the lady, "I think I'm still a rotten speller, and must have made a mistake."

"I think," said the man, "you shouldn't have gone on about wanting a child, a child."

"Perhaps I shouldn't," she said. "But, now I've got so many, what do I do?"

"Well, you can always visit me," he said, "I've only got that crooked cat and that crooked mouse, so there'll just be the three of us in my crooked little house."

"Well, I might visit," she said.

"And she probably did. Particularly when – with all those children – she didn't know what to do.

# Oh

# Tweedle!

Old King Cole was as merry as ever.

"Hurry up there; I want my fiddlers," he shouted merrily.

"And I'd like my bowl," he shouted, even more merrily.

"And I'd certainly like my pipe," he shouted louder still, and just as merrily.

The three fiddlers did as they were told. So did the pipe-man and the bowl-man who had to carry these things. They had all done it a hundred times before, a thousand times before, and didn't mind the work so much as that confounded merriment. To begin with King Cole had made them merry, as he was always in such a good mood. But after a while, as he went on being merry, day after day, month after month, this began to get on their nerves.

"Yo, ho, ho," the king would chuckle, as merry as ever. "Ha, ha, ha, hee, hee, hee."

"Why has it always got to be ho-ho, ha-ha, and hee-hee?" said the fiddlers.

"Why can't he ever say anything else?"

"Well, you can't if you're being merry," said the pipe-man. "All you can say is Ho and Ha and Hee and that's all he does say."

"The other day I dropped the bowl," said the bowl-man, "and, instead of taking me by the left leg, and throwing me down the stairs, he was just merry. 'Ho, ho, the bowl is broke,' was all he said, and merrily told me to get another one."

"I would have thought our music was enough to take the smile off his face," said a fiddler. "Although each of us has a very fine fiddle, and very fine fiddles

have we, we only go twee-tweedle-dee, tweedle-dee. You can't get much less merry than that."

"I've never dared to say that," said the pipe-man. "But it always is twee-tweedle-dee, tweedle-dee from you fiddlers."

For a moment the fiddlers looked angry, and even less merry than normal, but they had to agree. Their fiddles were fine, and deserved a better fate. But, if Old King Cole wanted twee-tweedle-dee, tweedle-dee, so be it. And if that kept him merry he was either deaf or daft, probably a bit of both.

"So what can we do?" asked a fiddler.

"I think there's nothing for it," said another, "but to make him less merry. Then we could play good music to cheer him up."

"So how," asked the third fiddler, "do we make him less cheerful, less smiling-all-the-time, less merry?"

The three fiddlers thought. So did the pipe-man and the bowl-man.

They all looked gloomily at each other, as they couldn't come up with an answer. At that moment King Cole looked at them.

"So what's with you lot?" he shouted merrily. "You look like yesterday's baked beans," and he chuckled merrily.

"Cheer up," he went on, "it probably won't happen," and his whole face creased from side to side in a fit of merriment.

"Let's have some fiddling," he called, "and my pipe, and my bowl. I can't stand anyone not being merry."

So the fiddlers tweed and deed and tweedled, and then had an idea. If he couldn't stand unmerriment, why not give him lots of it, lots and lots of it from all sorts of unmerry people. That would surely make him sad. What a great idea!

When they had tweed and tweedled sufficiently, and the King had gone off to bed – merrily, the fiddlers stayed up late, thinking of all the people they knew fairly guaranteed to be unmerry.

"Well, there's Jack and Jill," one said. "Breaking your crown probably makes you unmerry for quite a time, even if you do mend your head with vinegar and brown paper, and Jack and Jill do fall down every time they fetch a pail of water."

"Put them on the list," said another, "as I can't believe they're merry. What about Doctor Foster? From what I hear of him he is always stepping in puddles right up to his middle, and that must make him a sorry soul. He'll do his bit to damp down our King Cole, I'm sure."

"Great," said the third fiddler, "and then there's Little Johnny Green, who puts pussies into wells, and I can't believe he's happy. And we mustn't forget

Georgy Porgy. Not only do girls cry when he kisses them, but he always runs away from the boys. So he loses both ways, and just can't be merry. George may not make the Old King cry, but should remove some of that awful day-in, day-out, morning-noon-and-night merriment."

"I've got the best of them all," said the first fiddler, interrupting. "You can't be merry if you've got no food. And you certainly can't if there's not even any for your dog. Fancy having nothing, absolutely nothing in your cupboard. Fancy even bothering to put a bone there, and how depressing it must be to find that you don't have that bone when you next look. Or rather your dog doesn't. Old Mother Hubbard has just got to come."

The three fiddlers jumped around with glee. They even took up their fiddles to fiddle a jig, and were delighted with the list they had written down. There was Jack, Jill, Dr Foster, Johnny Green, Georgy Porgy, Mrs Hubbard. For good measure they then added the Old Man who couldn't say his prayers.

"Can't be much fun being thrown down stairs," said someone; "So he should be good and glum."

"Then there's the Three Bears," said someone else; "They make an awful fuss whenever a girl lies on their beds or eats some of their porridge. Anyone who makes that amount of fuss must be, ha, like a bear with a sore head."

The others laughed, just a little, but added the Old Man and all Three Bears to the list. So there was now Jack, Jill, Dr Foster, Johnny Green, Georgy

Porgy, Mrs Hubbard, Old Man, and Three Bears, making ten in all to see the King. Surely that lot will take the grin off his face and make him a bit more normal.

The fiddlers decided to invite the ten very special guests to a party. Then, after everyone was assembled, they would ask the King to join them. When confronted by such an assortment of unmerriment he would be bound to lose that perpetual, gaping, grinning, boring smile of his. He even had it when he got up in the morning. And when he had to take medicine. And when his boiled eggs were only half done. And when the bath water went cold. And when he stubbed his toe or got stung by a wasp.

"Oh, little waspy," he would say, "now you've made me forget about my stubbed toe, and that made me forget about my cold bath, and that made me forget about the egg, and so thank you little waspy because you've made me just as merry as ever."

With that he would guffaw loudly, show all his teeth even more than usual, and make the fiddlers wonder, not for the first time, if they couldn't find a job somewhere else.

Everyone had been invited for three o'clock, and at three exactly there was a knock on the door. It was the Old Man.

"I thought I'd better set off in good time," he said, "because I am a bit old and also sore from being thrown downstairs so often."

He did look wonderfully sad and the fiddlers welcomed him into the party room. Then came Dr Foster, dripping wet up to his middle, and none too pleased with life.

"I'll never go to Gloucester again," he muttered, and went to chat with the Old Man.

Mother Hubbard was next. She looked tremendously miserable but, better still, had brought her dog. This looked sad, and thin, and as hangdog as could be. The Three Bears were just as good, moaning about a lack of porridge, a disturbed night and what they might do to one little girl should they ever find her.

Jack and Jill staggered in next, each looking a sorry sight. She was limping badly, and he had a lot of vinegar and brown paper all over his head. Surely, thought the fiddlers, surely this pair alone would make the Old King swap his smile and merriment for a somewhat sadder look.

"We never did get the water," said Jack, moaning
quietly.

"Not a drop in our pail," added Jill, moaning rather
louder.

Johnny Green and Georgy Porgy came in together.
They were wondering, noisily, why everyone was
against them. They were always being got at. It
wasn't fair.

"After all," said Johnny, "I'm not the first person to
be unkind to a cat, and that wretched Tommy Stout
goes around everywhere saying how he fished poor
Pussy out, and I wish he'd shut up."

Georgy Porgy was similarly upset.

"Shouldn't girls *be* kissed?" he said. "And why do
they have to boo-hoo all over the place whenever I do

kiss them? Of course I run away when a great gang comes after me. It just isn't fair, that's all."

The three fiddlers, and the bowl-man, and the pipe-man listened to this chat, and were delighted. It was just the sort of misery they wanted to hear. Plainly the two boys couldn't think about anything else. Not only were they being downight miserable but self-pitying as well. That was always enough to take the smile off anyone else's face.

"Come and have something to eat," said the fiddlers, and the boys slouched over to the food table. The five hosts were delighted with their ten guests. They looked round the room most contentedly. There was Jill listening to the Old Man telling her that his fall had been much more hurtful than hers.

"You weren't thrown down," he said.

The Three Bears were listening to the Hubbard dog.

"At least you had some porridge," said the dog, "and I don't have a bed of any kind."

Dr Foster had gone across to talk to Johnny Green.

"I think you should have been kinder to that cat," he said. "It's bad enough being half wet, but being wet through must be terrible."

"You see, no one does understand me," said Johnny to Georgy, "it's all so unfair."

The five hosts thought this was exactly the right time to fetch King Cole. Everybody looked as sad as anything. Self-pity was all over the place. The party was going like a wet blanket. It was just what they had wanted.

"Let's call the King," they agreed.

"At least it makes a change from him calling us the whole time," said a fiddler, laughing.

"No laughing," said another fiddler. "We don't want to encourage him."

It has to be admitted that the King was amazed when he entered the party room. He had never met any of the three men, two boys, two women and four animals who were gathered there, but he had heard of all of them, their exploits being quite famous.

"Good heavens," thought the King to himself, "so that's what Mrs Hubbard looks like, and her dog, and those three different sized bears."

At first he got the Old Man muddled up with Dr Foster, and even Georgy with Johnny, but they were all sorted out after he had been introduced. Besides, he saw Georgy trying to plant a kiss on Jill's bruised cheek, and that helped, particularly after Jack had come running up to stop him.

"Wonderful," said Old King Cole, putting a brave face on it all. "How nice of you to come. Fiddlers, let's have some music."

"Twee-tweedle-dee, tweedle-dee," went the fiddlers as they wondered if their trick was going to succeed. Would the King swap his smile for a more ordinary look?

Just then they saw the Hubbard dog gobbling up a great plateful of food, and looking tremendously happy. Mrs H. herself was also gobbling, and looking happier still.

"Oh dear," thought the fiddlers, "that isn't right."

The King then called for his nurse, a call the fiddlers had never heard before. She came in and started to attend to the wounded guests, Jack, Jill, and the Old Man. She also arranged a dry pair of trousers for Dr Foster. As for the Bears they were given the three comfiest chairs in the whole Palace *and* great platefuls of porridge.

Meanwhile a tremendous quantity of food was slipping down the throats of Johnny Green and Georgy Porgy.

"Perhaps life isn't so bad after all," the two of them said to each other. "This chocolate cake really is scrumptious."

A quite terrible thing then happened. The King, who had been looking puzzled, and who had then been busy calling for the nurse and arranging for more food, started to smile. It was only a little smile at first but it got bigger and bigger. Eventually he was beaming across the room in his standard, horrible, ghastly merry way.

"What a wonderful, happy, exciting day this is," he shouted, ever so merrily.

"Oh tweedle!" said the fiddlers. There was really nothing else to say.

# *Some other* Jackanory *titles:*

## DAISY PIG
*M.J. Robson*

When Daisy Pig hears how fashionable it is to get a tan, she buys herself a bikini and takes her first trip to the seaside. Unfortunately, Daisy falls asleep in the sun. When she wakes up not only has she turned bright pink but there is a faint bacony smell in the air and people are looking at her in a very strange way . . . 'Daisy Pig at the Seaside' is just one of five delightful stories about an extremely confident lady pig.

## JONNY BRIGGS AND THE JUNIOR TENNIS
*Joan Eadington*

Jonny Briggs had never thought of playing tennis, not even when he hears that the school is to have its first ever tennis courts. But after his dog Razzle finds a very, very ancient and extremely smelly tennis ball, Jonny decides he will enter the competition – maybe even become a Junior Tennis star . . .

## BEST FRIENDS
*Anthony Smith*

How do friends become friends? Is it because they live next door? Or because they don't live next door? Or because everyone else is so beastly? *Best Friends* tells stories about friendship, all set around the time of the Great Flood, when Noah built his Ark and filled it with two of every kind of animal. From aardvarks to zorillas, kangaroos and koalas, everyone needs Best Friends.

## BOGGART SANDWICH
*Martin Riley*

Boggarts are bold, busy, witty, poetic and outlandish creatures of fantasy. Their weird and wonderful tales range from the megalithic to the mechanical and the modern, sometimes in the same paragraph. Boggarts live at the edge of our lives. Perhaps you'd like to know them better . . .